Kindness

is my

Superpower

A children's Book About Empathy, Kindness and Compassion

Alicia Ortego

This Book is dedicated to my beloved Grandmother & Mother.

Their love and kindness have been my source of inspiration.

~ AO

I'm Lucas, just an ordinary **boy**,
And this is Teddy, my favourite **toy**.

I like to eat sweets, jellies, and **cakes**,
But sometimes I make some **mistakes**.

You see, yesterday, I was in a very bad **mood,**
So sadly, I did something extremely **rude.**

I teased my friend, Lisa, for wearing **glasses**,
It made her cry for the rest of her **classes**.

When I got home, I was greeted by my **mum**,
I was sad to see her face looking **glum**.

"Honey, you made your friend, Lisa, **cry**,
Hurting people's feelings is wrong. Do you know **why**?"

"You should always be kind," my dear mother **said**,
I knew I'd done wrong, so I bowed my **head**.

"What does it mean to be kind?" I **implored**,
Mum hugged me tightly; when she did, my heart **soared**.

"Kindness is shown when
you say a gentle **word**,

Be kind to your sister,
and even a **bird**.

You can be kind to someone
who makes you **mad**,

You can be kind to someone
who is feeling **sad**."

"Be kind and respect those who are older than **you**,
Show respect and kindness to younger ones **too**.

Kindness is shown helping someone in **need**,
And kindness is shown when you do a good **deed**."

I pondered her words and couldn't sleep all **night**,
I wanted to be kind and genuinely **polite**.

So, right then and there, without any **warning**,
I decided to become very kind in the **morning**.

And, in the morning, the first thing I did **do**,
When mum made me breakfast, I told her, "**Thank you**."

I changed out of my pajamas
warm, soft and **red**,

I put away my toys
and made my own **bed**.

On the bus, I behaved the best as could **be**,
I even asked the new boy to sit next to **me**.

At school, I helped him find his classroom **too**,
I knew it was the very least I could **do**.

I said, "Good morning," to all of my **friends**,
I even shared my brand new crayons and **pens**.

Then I saw Lisa; her eyes still looked **sad**,
I approached her slowly, still feeling **bad**.

"I'm sorry I teased you," I said with bent **head**.
Lisa gave me a smile. "It's okay," she **said**.

I realized that kindness is really super **cool**,
So, I was also kind when I got out of **school**.

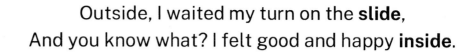

Outside, I waited my turn on the **slide**,
And you know what? I felt good and happy **inside**.

I was patient and kind, not angry at **all**,
And I even found joy helping a boy find his **ball**.

I picked up the rubbish, even though it wasn't **mine**.
Kindness and doing good deeds made my heart **shine**.

I loved going shopping
with mum to buy **food**,

Holding open doors
put me in such a good **mood**.

And after we bought my favourite toy and a **treat**,
Mum and I helped an old lady cross the **street**.

I continued to be kind, with joy and with **glee**,
Watching dad fall asleep in front of the **TV**.

He was sleeping on the sofa instead of his **bed**,
So, I covered him with a blanket and kissed his **forehead**.

I helped my little sister tie her **shoelace**,
I was glad to see the big smile on her **face**.

Being kind is amazing for everyone's **sake**,
Like giving your neighbour a yummy piece of **cake**.

I like to help mine water his **flowers**,
It really seems kindness has magical **powers**!

I no longer do mean things like **before**,
I don't tease others and I don't slam the **door**.

I stopped being selfish, and I share all my **toys**,
I don't shout out loud or make too much **noise**.

Kindness is something anyone can **learn**:
Give to others and ask nothing in **return**.

Helping others is simply the best thing to **do**.
When you are kind, kindness comes back to **you**.

Acts of kindness

A random act of kindness is an unexpected act of kindness done by one person for another without any way to have predicted it. Doing acts of kindness is one of the best activities parents can do with their kids. It's a great way to bond as a family, a lot of fun and teaches kids about compassion and service. Any act of kindness no matter how big or small can make a difference - especially when done intentionally.

Simple Acts of Kindness Ideas

Leave someone a kind note	Give a compliment	**Hold the door open for someone**	Do a chore for a sibling	**Create care packages**
Bring dinner to someone	**Donate old books**	Smile	**Clean up your room without being asked**	Give a candy bar to the bus driver
Tell a family member how much you love them	Help make dinner	**Free space**	Pick up litter	**Give a hug**
Let someone go ahead of you	**Volunteer**	Say thank you when you see service members	**Bake cookies for firefighters or police**	Write a thank you letter

Author's note:

Thank you so much for purchasing this book and for meeting Lucas. If you enjoyed it, please consider leaving a review or recommending it to a friend.

Visit my website for more information
www.aliciaortego.com

Thank you again for your support!

~ **Alicia Ortego**

Scan the code below to get your free gift now!

"*As we work to create light for others,
we naturally light our own way.*"

~ **Mary Anne Radmacher**

Made in United States
North Haven, CT
02 January 2022

14097547R00022